DOO GOOD TOGETHER, SCOOBY-DOO!

CAPSTONE EDITIONS
a capstone imprint

Doo Good Together, Scooby-Doo! is published by Capstone Editions
a Capstone Imprint
1710 Roe Crest Drive
North Mankato, Minnesota 56003
www.capstonepub.com

CAPS41973

Printed in the United States of America.
PA70

Library of Congress Cataloging-in-Publication data
Names: Jones, Christianne C., author.
Title: Doo good together, Scooby-Doo! / by Christianne Jones.
Description: North Mankato, Minnesota : Capstone Editions, [2019] | Series: Scooby-Doo! Scooby-Doo! |
Summary: "When Crystal Cove's mayor asks for help, Scooby-Doo and the gang work together to Doo Good in their community"—Provided by publisher.
Identifiers: LCCN 2019002575| ISBN 9781684461080 (hardcover) | ISBN 9781684461097 (eBook pdf)
Classification: LCC PZ7.J6823 Doo 2019 | DDC [E]—dc23
LC record available at https://lccn.loc.gov/2019002575

Editor: Christopher Harbo
Designer: Hilary Wacholz

SCOOBY-DOO!™ DOO GOOD

Scooby-Doo and his friends are teaming up to inspire, equip, and mobilize kids and families to create meaningful change in their communities! It's all about DOO-ing the right thing—a message at the heart of Scooby-Doo since its inception. Learn more at ScoobyDooGood.com.

"What's going on?" Fred asked.

"We'd like to thank you for your service to our community," the mayor declared. "Your crime-solving skills make Crystal Cove a better place."

"You're welcome," Daphne said. "We love to Doo Good."

"Jinkies! Maybe all those cars are a clue," Velma exclaimed.

"Like, there's only one way to find out," Shaggy said. "Let's go inside."

"So why did the mayor call us?" Velma asked. "She had plenty of volunteers today."

"I don't know," Fred said. "Let's pay her a visit to get to the bottom of this mystery."

"This food is going to help a lot of people in need," Daphne explained.

"And with all of us working together, we'll have it organized and ready in no time," Fred said.

"Double yummy!" Shaggy said.

"There's no time to eat, guys," Fred said. "We have food to donate."

At the food bank, the gang was surprised once again by what they saw.

"Zoinks! Like, am I imagining things, or is that line really long?" Shaggy asked.

"It sure is," Velma said. "The mayor must not have known so many volunteers would show up."

"Like, sorry, sir," Shaggy apologized. "This dog already has a home."

"But this pup still needs one," Velma said, pointing out a cute puppy.

"Looks like we're done here, Scoob," Shaggy said. "Let's go check out the food bank!"

Soon the gang's work in the shelter was nearly done.

"Dad! Can I keep him?" a young girl cried, hugging Scooby-Doo.

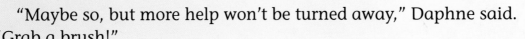

"Maybe we have a mystery on our hands after all," Fred said.

"Maybe so, but more help won't be turned away," Daphne said. "Grab a brush!"

But at the pet shelter, the gang found many volunteers already hard at work.

"I'm confused," Velma said. "It doesn't look like the pet shelter needs help either."

"That takes care of the park," Daphne said. "What's next?"

"The pet shelter," Fred answered. "It's adoption day, and the shelter and animals need to be in tip-top shape."

"Everything is more fun as a team," Daphne agreed.
"Especially when you are helping others."

"'Meddling' again? Can't anyone think of another way to describe us?" Daphne asked.

"Like curious, snoopy, prying—" Velma started to say.

"It doesn't matter," said Fred. "Our job is to solve mysteries, and that's what we do."

"Like, right on!" Shaggy cheered.

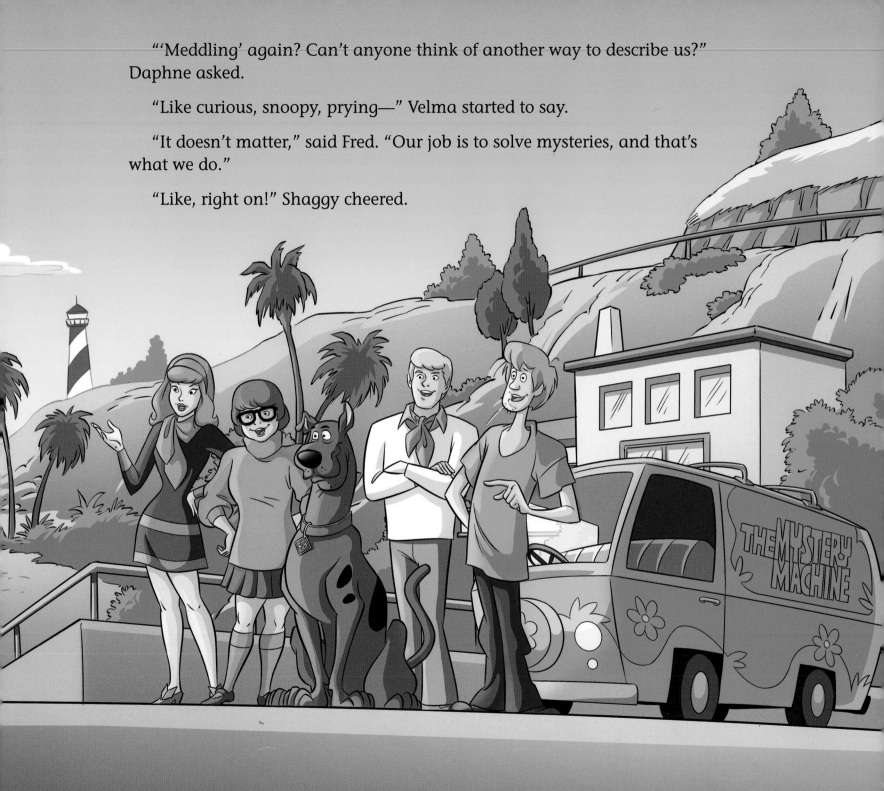

The Mystery Inc. gang had solved another mystery, but they had no time to go back and rest at their headquarters.

"Hey, gang. I just got off the phone with the mayor," Fred said.

"What's going on?" Velma asked.

"She doesn't have enough volunteers to help at Crystal Cove's park, pet shelter, and food bank," Fred replied.

"Well, it's no mystery," Daphne said. "But helping our community is just as important."

"Like, I agree," Shaggy said. "But I'll need a snack first."

"You can grab a Scooby Snack in the Mystery Machine," Velma replied. "It's time to Doo Good."

"Jeepers!" Daphne exclaimed. "Look at all the people cleaning up the park."

"That's odd," Velma said. "I thought the mayor didn't have enough volunteers."

"You can never have too many helping hands," Fred said.
"Let's get to work!"

"Like, picking up trash isn't so bad when you do it with friends," Shaggy said.

DOO GOOD TOGETHER, SCOOBY-DOO!

WRITTEN BY
CHRISTIANNE JONES

ILLUSTRATED BY
COMICUP DESIGN STUDIO SL

"That takes care of the park," Daphne said. "What's next?"

"The pet shelter," Fred answered. "It's adoption day, and the shelter and animals need to be in tip-top shape."

"Everything is more fun as a team," Daphne agreed.
"Especially when you are helping others."